THREE *MORE* STORIES

You Can Read
to Your CAT

Sara Swan Miller   *ILLUSTRATED BY* **True Kelley**

sandpiper

HOUGHTON MIFFLIN HARCOURT
Boston New York

For Marty, Erin, and
Henry the Grandcat
—S.S.M.

For Chuck the Cat
—T.K.

Text copyright © 2002 by Sara Swan Miller
Illustrations copyright © 2002 by True Kelley

SANDPIPER and the SANDPIPER logo are trademarks of Houghton Mifflin Harcourt
Publishing Company.

For information about permission to reproduce selections from this book, write to trade.permissions@
hmhco.com or to Permissions, Houghton Mifflin Harcourt Publishing Company, 3 Park Avenue, 19th
Floor, New York, New York 10016.

www.hmhco.com.

The text of this book is set in 16-point Baskerville Book.
The illustrations are ink and watercolor.

The Library of Congress has cataloged the hardcover edition as follows:
Miller, Sara Swan.
Three more stories you can read to your cat/by Sara Swan Miller;
illustrated by True Kelley.
p. cm.
Summary: Stories addressed to cats and written from a cat's point of view,
featuring such topics as birthday presents, snow, and breakfast.
[1. Cats—Fiction.] I. Kelley, True, ill. II Title.
PZ7.M63344Tf 2002
[Fic]—dc21
2001039255

ISBN: 978-0-618-11035-3 hardcover
ISBN: 978-0-547-74448-3 paperback

Manufactured in China
LEO 10 9 8 7 6 5 4 3 2
4500678939

CONTENTS

Introduction

Most cats sleep a lot. Does yours? Why *do* cats sleep so much? Maybe they just get bored.

When you are bored, what do you do? You can always read a good book. But cats never do learn to read, even a smart one like yours.

Do you want to do a nice thing for your cat? You can read these stories out loud. Cats always like to hear stories about themselves.

Ask your cat to come sit on your lap and hear a story. Ask very nicely. Never tell a cat what to do!

Remember to pet your cat while you read. Your cat likes that, too.

Here kitty, kitty! Would you like to sit on my lap? Would you like to hear a story? You will like this one!

1

HAPPY BiRThDAY

ONE MORNING you were taking a nice nap on your favorite chair. Then, THUMP THUMP THUMPITY THUMP! Here came your friend clumping into the room.

"My friend is so noisy!" you said to yourself. "What is wrong with people, anyway?"

"Wake up, cat," said your friend. "It's your birthday!"

"So what?" you said to yourself. "I am busy.
I am very, very busy taking my nap."

"Look!" said your friend. "Presents! For you!"
You opened one eye. What was your friend
talking about?

"Let me open one for you," said your friend. Rustle, rustle, rustle. What a funny sound! You opened the other eye and jumped off your chair.

"Look!" said your friend. "A mouse! Here it comes!"

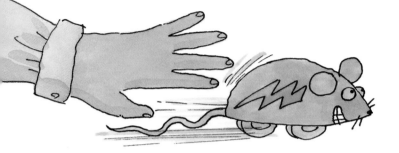

You pounced on the mouse.
You batted it across the floor
and chased after it.

The mouse just lay there.
You poked it with your paw.

"Run away, mouse!" you said.
But the mouse did not run away. It didn't
even move.

"This mouse is dead," you said to
yourself. "What a stupid present."
You jumped back on your chair.
A nap was much more interesting
than a dead mouse.

"Wait!" said your friend. "Here's another present!
Let me open it for you."
Rustle, rustle, rustle. What *was* that interesting
sound?

You opened your eyes again and jumped
off your chair.

"See?" said your friend. "A wind-up spider!"
Your friend let the spider go. Clackety clackety
clack! It came running right at you!
"YEOW!" you screamed.

You ran under the couch. But the scary spider chased after you.

You raced under a chair. But the scary spider found you again.

You leaped on top of the table.
"Go away, horrible spider!" you said.

Finally, the scary spider got tired. It lay down
and took a nap under the table. You waited
until it was fast asleep. Then you ran far, far
away, all the way to kitchen. You hid behind
the garbage can.
"I don't think I like birthdays," you said to
yourself.

CLUMP! CLUMP! CLUMP! Here came your
friend again.

"Don't you like your presents?" said your friend.
"Here, you will like this one."

Rustle, rustle, rustle. There was that interesting
sound again! You carefully crept out from behind
the garbage can.

"See?" said your friend. "A nice warm sweater!
Let me put it on you."

The next thing you knew, you were all wrapped up in a horrible hot rag.

"This is the worst present yet!" you said to yourself.

You clawed at the horrible rag.

You chewed at the edges.

Finally, you wiggled
your way out of it.

You rolled the rag into a ball and
shot it behind the garbage can.
Birthdays were awful!

No more presents!

"I'm sorry you don't like your presents, cat," said your friend. "I know! Do you want to play with the wrapping paper?"

Rustle, rustle, rustle. So *that* was that fun sound! You pounced on the Rustle. You batted it across the floor. You pounced on it again. The Rustle ran away. You pounced on it again and again and again. The Rustle ran this way, and that way, and this way, and that way.

Finally, you pounced on the Rustle one last time and chewed it to bits.

"Now THAT was a great present!" you said to yourself. "Maybe birthdays are not so bad after all."
But dopey dead mice and scary spiders and horrible rags and chasing Rustles can wear a cat out. You curled up in a warm patch of sun and went back to your nice nap.

Did you like that story, you good cat? Would you like to hear another? You will like this one, too.

2

FUNNY wHiTE STUFF

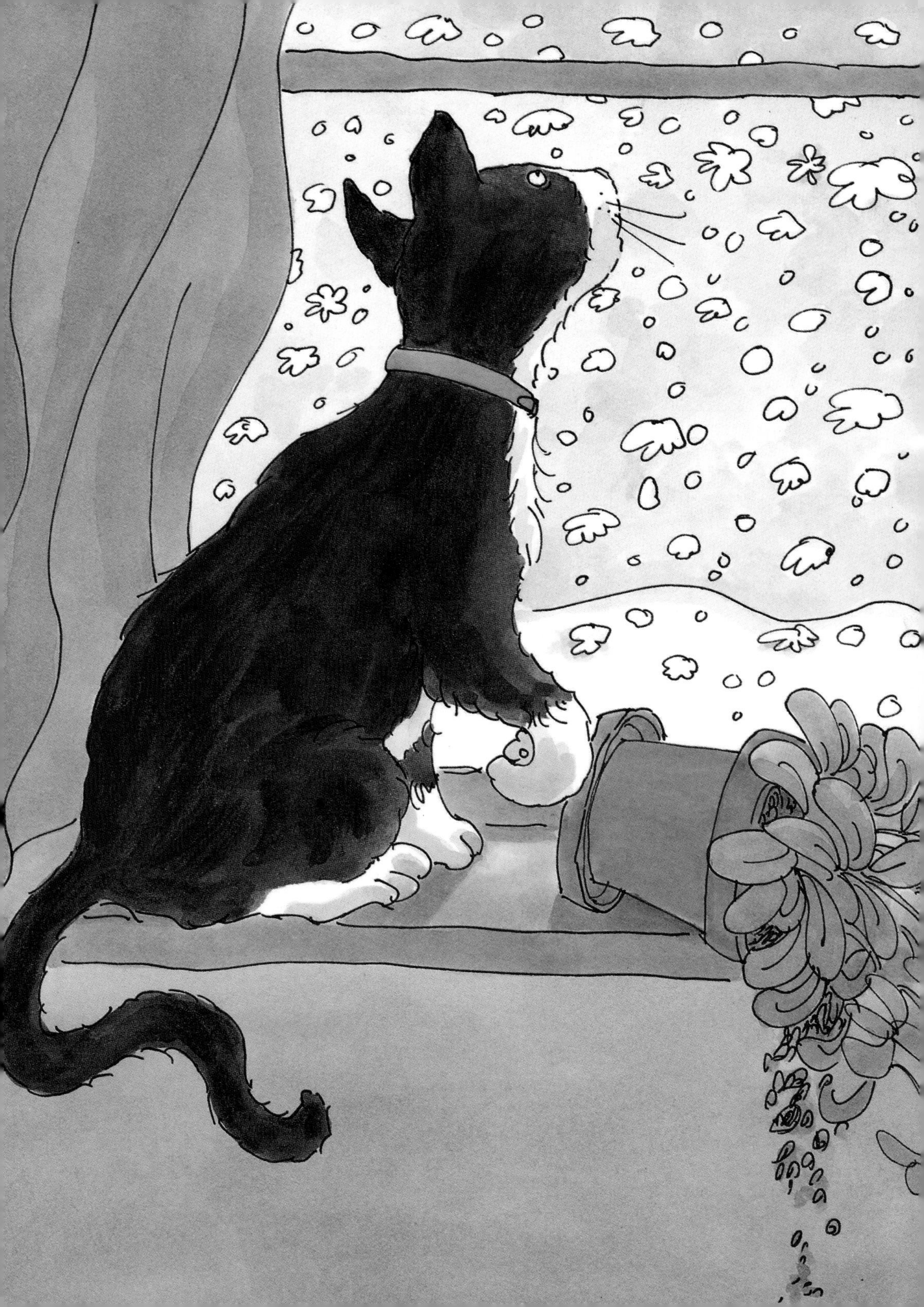

ONE DAY you were feeling bored. You were tired of taking naps. You were tired of cleaning your paws. You were tired, tired, tired of being in the house.

You jumped up on the window ledge and looked outside. Something funny was happening! Little white things were falling out of the sky. What was going on? It looked like fun!

You had to find out. You didn't want to miss out on Fun! You ran to the door.

"OUT!" you called. "Out, out, OUT, OUT!"
Finally, your friend came clumping over to help.

"OUT!" you said.

"Oh, no," said your friend. "You don't want to go out. It's snowing!"
Of course you wanted to go out! What did your silly friend know?

"Out!" you said again. "Out, out, OUT, OUT!"

"You won't like it out there," said your friend.

Oh, yes you *would* like it out there. Cats know
what cats like!

"OUT!" you said again.

You had to get out there. All the good Fun was
happening without you.

Your friend opened the door. At last! Fun! You stuck your nose out the open door. Little white things fell on your nose. They were cold and wet! More white things flew into your eyes. You could hardly see! You blinked and blinked and shook your head. But the little white things would not leave you alone.

Where was the ground? And what was this white
blanket lying where the ground should be? You
stuck in one paw. The white blanket was freezing!
And wet! You shook off your paw. You stuck in
your other paw. It was even colder and wetter!
This was no fun at all!

Why did your friend make you go outside in all this wet, cold white stuff? Your friend was so mean!

"In!" you said to the door. "In, in, IN, INNNNN!"

The door opened. You ran inside. Safe!
"I told you so," said your friend.
You stalked right past your friend. You held
your nose and your tail high.

You jumped up into your favorite chair.
"I will never talk to my mean friend again," you
said to yourself. "So there!"
A nice warm nap is much more fun than cold
white stuff. You curled up on your chair and fell
fast asleep.

Are you still there, good cat? Are you ready for another story? All right, this is the very last one.

3

BREAKFAST TIME

ONE MORNING you woke up extra early.
"I am so hungry!" you said to yourself. "Where is
my breakfast? Where is my friend with my food?"
You looked downstairs. You looked upstairs. There
was your friend in bed! You jumped up on the bed
and walked over your friend's tummy.

"Ugh," said your friend.

You walked over your friend's chest and onto
the pillow.
You dug your claws into your friend's hair.
You started making yourself a nice hair nest.

"Go away, cat!" said your friend. "It is
only six o'clock!"
Your friend pushed you off the bed.
"Phooey!" you said to yourself. "What can I do
until my lazy friend gets up?"

A little rug was lying on the floor.
You pounced on it with all four feet.

You pushed it across the floor.
You dug your claws into it
and made it into a ball.

You dived inside
and hid.

"Be quiet, cat," said your friend.
Your friend was so silly! Cats are always quiet!

You jumped up on the table.
Aha! A nice piece of crackly paper!
You pounced on it and chewed it
up into little bits. Then you shot the
bits around on the table.
"That was fun," you said to yourself.
"But now I am hungrier than ever!"

You jumped back on the bed. It was time for breakfast!
"Now!" you said. "Now! NOW!"
"Go away!" said your friend.
"Now!" you said. "NOW!"
Your friend pushed you off
the bed again. Some friend!

Wait! Something was following you! You turned around to pounce. But it was gone! You turned around the other way. You galloped around and around. And around and around. POUNCE! You caught it!

"Oh!" you said to yourself. "My tail!"
You gave it a good licking.

"Be quiet, cat!" said your friend. "I am sleeping."
You jumped back on the bed.
"Now!" you said. "NOW! NOW!"

But your friend did not get up. You jumped
back down.

"I guess I will have to find my own breakfast," you said to yourself.

You went prowling around the room. A jar! Maybe there was food inside! You knocked the jar over. Little glass balls went rolling all over the floor. They made a wonderful clattering noise!

Marbles

"What fun!" you said to yourself.
You chased after the little balls. You batted them
here and batted them there. You shot some under
the chair and shot some more under the bed.
You shot a whole bunch of them under the table.
What great fun!

Oh, good! Your friend was getting up at last! It was time for breakfast! You went downstairs and sat next to your bowl.

"Now?" you said. "NOW?"

You waited and waited. Finally, your friend filled your bowl. You sniffed at it. Then you took a bite and crunched it up.